The Real Story of Christmas

Directly from the Bible

Luke 1:26-38,   Matthew 1:18-24
Luke 2:1-20,   Matthew 2:1-13

The Nativity Book for Children and Little Kids with Two Text Versions – the Original Scripture-referenced Bible Storybook and the Simplified Classic Jesus' Birth Story

BY MAMTALK PUBLISHING

A Gift for

....

From

....

Date

....

Contents

Part 1. The Annunciation

Luke 1:26 - 38*
*A shortened version for younger children (the parts have been cut for simplicity)

The Visitation

Luke 1:26-33

The angel Gabriel was sent from God to a town called Nazareth to a virgin Mary betrothed to a man named Joseph. And coming to her, he said, "Hail, favored one! The Lord is with you."

Then the angel said to her, "Do not be afraid, Mary, for you have found favor with God. You will bear a son, and you shall name him Jesus. He will be great and called Son of the Most High."

The Visitation

Luke 1:26-33

26 In the sixth month, the angel Gabriel was sent from God to a town of Galilee called Nazareth, 27 to a virgin betrothed to a man named Joseph, of the house of David, and the virgin's name was Mary.

28 And coming to her, he said, "Hail, favored one! The Lord is with you."

29 But she was greatly troubled at what was said and pondered what sort of greeting this might be.

30 Then the angel said to her, "Do not be afraid, Mary, for you have found favor with God.

31 Behold, you will conceive in your womb and bear a son, and you shall name him Jesus.

32 He will be great and will be called Son of the Most High, and the Lord God will give him the throne of David his father, 33 and he will rule over the house of Jacob forever, and of his kingdom there will be no end."

Part 1. The Annunciation – Luke 1:26-38 *(continuation)
*A shortened version for younger children (the parts have been cut for simplicity)

The Immaculate Conception
Luke 1:34-38

But Mary said to the angel, "How can this be, since I have no husband?" And the angel said to her in reply, "The holy Spirit will come upon you, and the power of the Most High will overshadow you. Therefore the child to be born will be called holy, the Son of God.

Mary said, "Behold, I am the handmaid of the Lord. May it be done to me according to your word." Then the angel departed from her.

The Immaculate Conception

Luke 1:34-38

34 But Mary said to the angel, "How can this be, since I have no relations with a man?"

35 And the angel said to her in reply, "The holy Spirit will come upon you, and the power of the Most High will overshadow you. Therefore the child to be born will be called holy, the Son of God.

36 And behold, Elizabeth, your relative, has also conceived a son in her old age, and this is the sixth month for her who was called barren; 37 for nothing will be impossible for God."

38 Mary said, "Behold, I am the handmaid of the Lord. May it be done to me according to your word." Then the angel departed from her.

Nazareth

Part 2. Joseph's Dream

Matthew 1:18 - 24[*]

[*]A shortened version for younger children (the parts have been cut for simplicity)

Joseph's Dream

Matthew 1:18-24

The angel of the Lord appeared to Joseph in a dream and said, "Joseph, son of David, do not be afraid to take Mary your wife into your home. For it is through the holy Spirit that this child has been conceived in her. She will bear a son and you are to name him Jesus."

When Joseph awoke, he did as the angel of the Lord had commanded him and took his wife into his home.

Joseph's Dream

Matthew 1:18-24

18 Now this is how the birth of Jesus Christ came about. When his mother Mary was betrothed to Joseph, but before they lived together, she was found with child through the holy Spirit.

19 Joseph her husband, since he was a righteous man, yet unwilling to expose her to shame, decided to divorce her quietly.

20 Such was his intention when, behold, the angel of the Lord appeared to him in a dream and said, "Joseph, son of David, do not be afraid to take Mary your wife into your home. For it is through the holy Spirit that this child has been conceived in her. 21 She will bear a son and you are to name him Jesus, because he will save his people from their sins."

22 All this took place to fulfill what the Lord had said through the prophet: 23 "Behold, the virgin shall be with child and bear a son, and they shall name him Emmanuel," which means "God is with us."

24 When Joseph awoke, he did as the angel of the Lord had commanded him and took his wife into his home.

Part 3. Birth of Jesus and Shepherds

Luke 2:1 - 20*

*A shortened version for younger children (the parts have been cut for simplicity)

Travel to Bethlehem

Luke 2:1-5

In those days a decree went out that the whole world should be enrolled. So all went to be enrolled, each to his own town. And Joseph too went up from the town of Nazareth to the city of David that is called Bethlehem, because he was of the house and family of David, to be enrolled with Mary, his betrothed, who was with child.

Part 3
The Birth of Jesus and Shepherds
Luke 2:1-20*
*A full version for older children

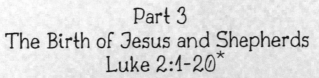

Travel to Bethlehem

Luke 2:1-5

1 In those days a decree went out from Caesar Augustus that the whole world should be enrolled.

2 This was the first enrollment, when Quirinius was governor of Syria.

3 So all went to be enrolled, each to his own town.

4 And Joseph too went up from Galilee from the town of Nazareth to Judea, to the city of David that is called Bethlehem, because he was of the house and family of David, 5 to be enrolled with Mary, his betrothed, who was with child.

Part 3. The Birth of Jesus and Shepherds - Luke 2:1-20[*] (continuation)
*A shortened version for younger children (the parts have been cut for simplicity)

Mary, Joseph, and Jesus
Luke 2:6-7

While they were there, the time came for her to have her child, and she gave birth to her firstborn son. She wrapped him in swaddling clothes and laid him in a manger, because there was no room for them in the inn.

Part 3 (continuation)
The Birth of Jesus and Shepherds - Luke 2:1-20*
*A full version for older children

Mary, Joseph, and Jesus

Luke 2:6-7

6 While they were there, the time came for her to have her child, 7 and she gave birth to her firstborn son. She wrapped him in swaddling clothes and laid him in a manger, because there was no room for them in the inn.

*A shortened version for younger children (the parts have been cut for simplicity)

The Angel and Shepherds
Luke 2:8-12

Now there were shepherds in that region living in the fields and keeping the night watch over their flock. The angel of the Lord appeared to them, and the glory of the Lord shone around them.

The angel said to them, "Do not be afraid; I proclaim to you good news of great joy. For today in the city of David a savior has been born for you who is Messiah and Lord. And this will be a sign for you: you will find an infant wrapped in swaddling clothes and lying in a manger."

Part 3 (continuation)
The Birth of Jesus and Shepherds - Luke 2:1-20*
*A full version for older children

The Angel and Shepherds

Luke 2:8-12

8 Now there were shepherds in that region living in the fields and keeping the night watch over their flock.

9 The angel of the Lord appeared to them and the glory of the Lord shone around them, and they were struck with great fear.

10 The angel said to them, "Do not be afraid; for behold, I proclaim to you good news of great joy that will be for all the people.

11 For today in the city of David a savior has been born for you who is Messiah and Lord.

12 And this will be a sign for you: you will find an infant wrapped in swaddling clothes and lying in a manger."

Part 3. The Birth of Jesus and Shepherds - Luke 2:1-20* (continuation)
*A shortened version for younger children (the parts have been cut for simplicity)

The Multitude of the Angels

Luke 2:13-14

And suddenly there was a multitude of the heavenly host with the angel, praising God and saying:

"Glory to God in the highest and on earth peace to those on whom his favor rests."

Part 3 (continuation)
The Birth of Jesus and Shepherds - Luke 2:1-20*
*A full version for older children

The Multitude of the Angels

Luke 2:13-14

13 And suddenly there was a multitude of the heavenly host with the angel, praising God and saying:

14 "Glory to God in the highest and on earth peace to those on whom his favor rests."

Part 3. The Birth of Jesus and Shepherds - Luke 2:1-20* (continuation)
*A shortened version for younger children (the parts have been cut for simplicity)

The Visit of the Shepherds
Luke 2:15-20

When the angels went away from them to heaven, the shepherds went in haste and found Mary and Joseph, and the infant lying in the manger. When they saw this, they made known the message that had been told them about this child.

Part 3 (continuation)
The Birth of Jesus and Shepherds - Luke 2:1-20*
*A full version for older children

The Visit of the Shepherds
Luke 2:15-20

15 When the angels went away from them to heaven, the shepherds said to one another, "Let us go, then, to Bethlehem to see this thing that has taken place, which the Lord has made known to us."

16 So they went in haste and found Mary and Joseph, and the infant lying in the manger.

17 When they saw this, they made known the message that had been told them about this child.

18 All who heard it were amazed by what had been told them by the shepherds.

19 And Mary kept all these things, reflecting on them in her heart.

20 Then the shepherds returned, glorifying and praising God for all they had heard and seen, just as it had been told to them.

Part 4. The Visit of the Magi
Matthew 2:1-12*
*A shortened version for younger children (the parts have been cut for simplicity)

King Herod and the Magi
Matthew 2:1-8

When Jesus was born in Bethlehem of Judea, in the days of King Herod, magi from the east arrived in Jerusalem, saying, "Where is the newborn king of the Jews? We saw his star at its rising and have come to do him homage."

When King Herod heard this, he was greatly troubled. Assembling all the chief priests and the scribes of the people, he inquired of them where the Messiah was to be born. They said to him, "In Bethlehem of Judea."

Then Herod sent the magi to Bethlehem and said, "Go and search diligently for the child. When you have found him, bring me word, that I too may go and do him homage."

Part 4 (continuation)
The Visit of the Magi – Matthew 2:1-13*
*A full version for older children

King Herod and the Magi
Matthew 2:1-8

1 When Jesus was born in Bethlehem of Judea, in the days of King Herod, behold, magi from the east arrived in Jerusalem, 2 saying, "Where is the newborn king of the Jews? We saw his star at its rising and have come to do him homage."

3 When King Herod heard this, he was greatly troubled, and all Jerusalem with him.

4 Assembling all the chief priests and the scribes of the people, he inquired of them where the Messiah was to be born.

5 They said to him, "In Bethlehem of Judea, for thus it has been written through the prophet: 6 'And you, Bethlehem, land of Judah, are by no means least among the rulers of Judah; since from you shall come a ruler, who is to shepherd my people Israel.'"

7 Then Herod called the magi secretly and ascertained from them the time of the star's appearance.

8 He sent them to Bethlehem and said, "Go and search diligently for the child. When you have found him, bring me word, that I too may go and do him homage."

Part 4. The Visit of the Magi – Matthew 2:1-13* (continuation)
*A shortened version for younger children (the parts have been cut for simplicity)

The Visit of the Magi
Matthew 2:9-12

After their audience with the king they set out. And behold, the star that they had seen at its rising preceded them, until it came and stopped over the place where the child was. And on entering the house they saw the child with Mary his mother. They prostrated themselves and did him homage. Then they opened their treasures and offered him gifts of gold, frankincense, and myrrh. And having been warned in a dream not to return to Herod, they departed for their country by another way.

Part 4 (continuation)
The Visit of the Magi – Matthew 2:1-13*
*A full version for older children

The Visit of the Magi

Matthew 2:9-12

9 After their audience with the king they set out. And behold, the star that they had seen at its rising preceded them, until it came and stopped over the place where the child was.

10 They were overjoyed at seeing the star, 11 and on entering the house they saw the child with Mary his mother. They prostrated themselves and did him homage. Then they opened their treasures and offered him gifts of gold, frankincense, and myrrh.

12 And having been warned in a dream not to return to Herod, they departed for their country by another way.

Part 4. The Visit of the Magi – Matthew 2:1-13* (continuation)
*A shortened version for younger children (the parts have been cut for simplicity)

The Flight to Egypt

Matthew 2:13

When they had departed, the angel of the Lord appeared to Joseph in a dream and said, "Rise, take the child and his mother, flee to Egypt, and stay there. Herod is going to search for the child."

Part 4 (continuation)
The Visit of the Magi – Matthew 2:1-13*
*A full version for older children

The Flight to Egypt

Matthew 2:13

13 When they had departed, behold, the angel of the Lord appeared to Joseph in a dream and said, "Rise, take the child and his mother, flee to Egypt, and stay there until I tell you. Herod is going to search for the child to destroy him."

The End!

So now you know the true story of Christmas and how the Savior of the world started his journey on Earth.

He came to the world to bring us love, joy, peace, and hope!

Practice and consolidation of the
Bible knowledge

Make up the Christmas Story using these pictures

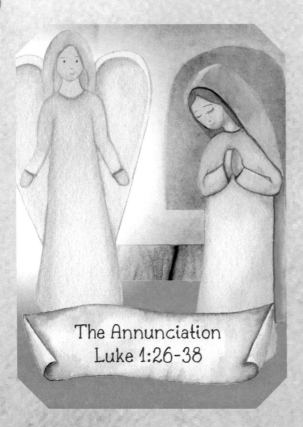

The Annunciation
Luke 1:26-38

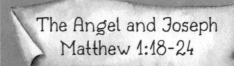

The Angel and Joseph
Matthew 1:18-24

Travel to Bethlehem
Luke 2:1-5

Mary, Joseph, and Jesus
Luke 2:6-7

Practice and consolidation of the Bible knowledge

Make up the Christmas Story using these pictures

The Angels and Shepherds
Luke 2:8-14

The Visit of the Shepherds
Luke 2:15-20

King Herod and the Magi
Matthew 2:1-8

The Visit of the Magi
Matthew 2:9-12

One day, an came to and told her

that she would have a special baby. was to

name the baby . and had to

travel to Bethlehem. rode on a .

While they were in Bethlehem, was born.

 and could not find a room at the inn,

so was born in a stable. There were

in the nearby fields taking care of their .

  Jesus   Mary   Joseph   Angel

Magi   Donkey   Sheep   Shepherds

An came to tell to that had

been born. Many 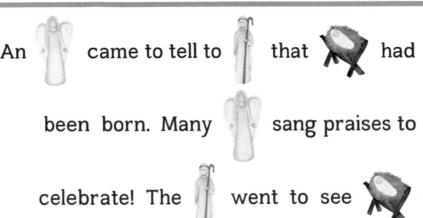 sang praises to

celebrate! The went to see .

They were amazed! The praised God and

hurried to tell everyone about the

Savior's birth. followed the star

to the manger and brought gifts

to .

Jesus   Mary   Joseph   Angel

Magi   Donkey   Sheep   Shepherds

Merry Christmas!

If you can spare a few minutes to leave us a review, we'd be super grateful!

Books for Kids by
MamTalk Publishing

Made in the USA
Middletown, DE
08 November 2023

42229237R00018